*For my sweet daughters, Alice and Emily, who bring
imagination to life. I love you with all my heart.*
—C.H.S.

For my mother and grandma
—H.N.

ACKNOWLEDGMENT:
*Special thanks to my daughter Alice, whose precious
childhood drawings inspired this story.*
—C.H.S.

Mommy in My Pocket

BY **Carol Hunt Senderak** 🦋 ILLUSTRATIONS BY **Hiroe Nakata**

HYPERION BOOKS FOR CHILDREN
NEW YORK

When school begins that one fall day,
I'll miss my mommy in every way.

I could put Mommy's picture in a locket,

but I would love to take her in my pocket.

What if I saw a shooting star fall,
and wished for my mommy to be small?

Into my pocket, I'd tuck Mommy just right,
not too loose, and not too tight.

Safe in my pocket, she would be,

then off to school, my mommy and me.

All day long, we would never part,
Mommy in my pocket, near my beating heart.

Mommy and I would have lunch at noon,
sharing chicken soup with my favorite spoon!

I'd whisper softly as the day went on,
"I'm so happy you're here with me, Mom."

At playtime, I would run about,
watching my pocket so Mommy wouldn't fall out.

Then school would end for Mommy and me—

time to go home to our family.

I would love every day to be just like this—
Mommy in my pocket would be my wish.

Yet when school starts, I know I'll be okay,
because the love in Mommy's hug and kiss . . .
will stay with me all day!